EEK!
STORIES TO MAKE YOU SHRIEK!

1. Fly Trap
2. Dragon Breath
3. Creep Show
4. The Bad Luck Penny
5. The Mummy's Gold
6. The Wax Museum
7. A Very Strange Doll's House
8. The Haunted Bike

EEK!
STORIES TO MAKE YOU SHRIEK!

Creep Show

Jennifer Dussling

Illustrated by Simon Cooper

MACMILLAN CHILDREN'S BOOKS

First published 1996 by Putnam & Grosset Group, USA

This edition published 1999 by Macmillan Children's Books
a division of Macmillan Publishers Limited
25 Eccleston Place, London SW1W 9NF
Basingstoke and Oxford

Associated companies throughout the world

ISBN 0 330 37130 4

Text copyright © Jennifer Dussling 1996
Illustrations copyright © Simon Cooper 1999

The right of Jennifer Dussling and Simon Cooper to be identified as the
author and illustrator of this work has been asserted by them in accordance
with the Copyright, Designs and Patents Act 1988.

135798642

A CIP catalogue record for this book is available from the British Library.

Printed and bound in Great Britain by Mackays of Chatham plc, Kent

Kids stay away from the old Star Movie Palace.

The story is that some guy died in there.

He got scared to death by a horror film.

I don't know if it's true or not. But the Star gives me the creeps. I have to pass it every day on my way home.

I always walk on the other side of the road.

But today I saw a sign outside –
FREE FILM TODAY. A free film!
Was this for real?

I crossed the road to get a closer
look.

The film was called *Superball*. I
had never heard of it. But I love
football. This was too good to
pass up.

I started to push the door. But it
swung open – all by itself!

Weird.

Inside it was dark and spooky. All the seats were very dusty.

You would think that with a free film the place would be packed. But no one else was there – just me.

A bag of popcorn was on one of the seats.

It was like it was put there just for me.

Then the film started. It was about a non-league team.

They weren't any good – just like my team!

The crowd was yelling something

at a kid in goal.

I play in goal too.

The kid turned around.

It was me!

All of a sudden, there was a

WHOOOSH! And I felt dizzy.

I shook my head and looked

around.

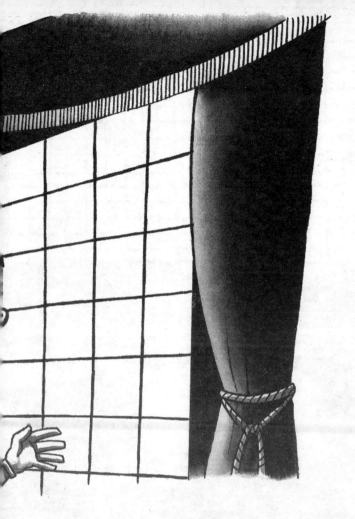

I was on the pitch, standing in goal!

I was not watching a film any more.

I was *in* the film!

A kid from the other team was coming in to take a penalty.

The crowd went silent.

CRACK!

The striker looped the ball over the heads of the other players.

Then it soared through the air towards the goal. Towards me!

It was just the kind of ball I never catch.

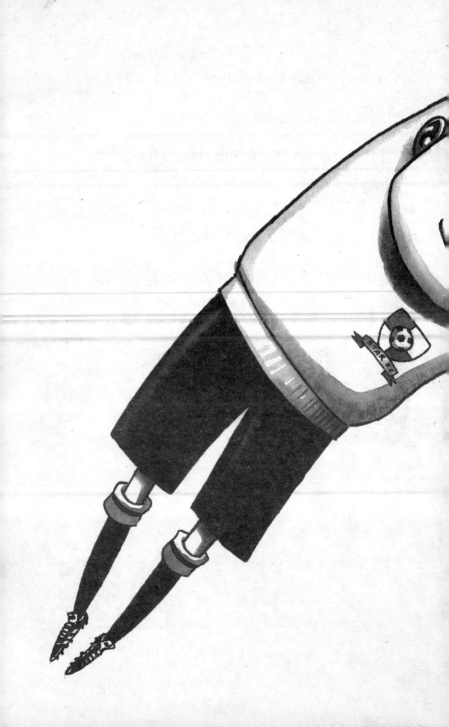

But this time I sprang into the air.
I stretched out my hands. I held my
breath.

And I caught it!

The whistle went.

The final ball!

I saved the match!

It was my dream come true.

Kids lifted me up.

Everybody was cheering.

Then the lights came on. I blinked.

I was back in the cinema.

Back in my seat.

I walked out in a daze. Had this really happened?

I started walking home.

Then I noticed it.

There were grass stains on my jeans!

The next day at school I
started to tell my friends about
the Star. But I stopped.

They would probably think I was
nuts. And somehow I felt this was
my secret.

Somehow this was meant just
for me.

That afternoon I had a piano
lesson. So I couldn't go to the Star.

But the next day I went back.
Was there going to be another
free film?

Yes! The film was called *Surf's Up!*

I have always wanted to surf.

I knew I should go home.

I had a ton of homework.

But I felt like the Star was pulling me – like a magnet.

I had to see if I was going to be in the film again.

I went inside. This time there was a Loadsanuts on one of the seats.

Loadsanuts are my favourite chocolate bars.

It really was put there just for me!

Then the film started. It was about surfers.

They were watching another kid surf.

They said how cool he looked.

I got a tingly feeling.

I was pretty sure I knew who they were talking about.

Me.

WHOOOSH!

Like magic, I was in the film again.

It was like I had been surfing my whole life.

But all of a sudden a huge wave knocked me off my surfboard.

I wiped out!

Over and over I tumbled in the water.

My arm scraped across my board.

Ow! That hurt!

I struggled out of the water.

But what do you know?

I wasn't at the beach any more!

I was back in the cinema – back in my seat.

What was going on here?

I ran out of the cinema and down the street. Then I passed a shop window and stopped. I saw myself in the glass.

My hair was wet.

And I was sunburnt.

How could I get sunburn from a film?

But it *was* sunburn.

And it hurt.

My arm hurt too. I didn't want to look at it. I didn't want to see what I knew I would see.

Finally I peered down and saw the horrible truth.

There were cuts and scrapes from my wipe-out.

Uh-oh.

This was a little scary.

Maybe *more* than a little scary. I got sunburnt in a dark cinema. I cut my arm.

I got hurt in a film.

And it was only a surf film!

What if it had been a murder mystery?

Or a war story?

Or a western?

Or, worst of all, a horror film?

I ran all the way home.

I didn't stop until I got to my room.

I was scared.

There was no way I was going back to the Star.

Who knew what could happen next time?

At dinner my mum looked at me strangely.

"Gosh, your face is red," she said. "You must have a temperature."

She felt my forehead.

"No school for you tomorrow."

So the next day I stayed at home.

No school is usually great.

Not this time.

I tried to read a book.

I tried to play a video game.

But all I could think about was the Star.

After lunch my mum went
shopping.

I was all alone.

Uh-oh.

I tried not to go.

But something was pulling me –

pulling me to the Star.

I grabbed my coat.

In ten minutes I was there.

The poster said *The Sweet Factory*.
Now that sounded like fun!
The worst thing that could happen
to me was a tummy ache!

Oh, no!

I had to get out!

I ran to the door.

It was locked!

Slowly, I turned around.

The film was starting and

WHOOOOOOSH!

I was in it.

The ground started to shake.

What was that?

Then I saw them . . .

Really big, green spiders with really
big fangs!
They were coming towards me!
I started to run.

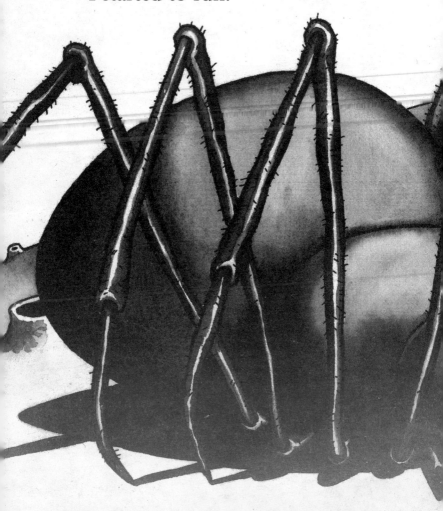

Maybe I would be lucky.

Maybe I could get away.

Maybe this wasn't . . .